U.S. HISTORY IN REVIEW

Congress of the United States
begun and held at the City of New-York, on
Wednesday the Fourth of March, one thousand seven hundred and eighty nine

The Bill of Rights

BY KATHRYN WALTON

Enslow PUBLISHING

Please visit our website, www.enslow.com. For a free color catalog of all our high-quality books, call toll free 1-800-398-2504 or fax 1-877-980-4454.

Cataloging-in-Publication Data
Names: Walton, Kathryn.
Title: The bill of rights / Kathryn Walton.
Description: Buffalo, New York: Enslow, 2024. | Series: U.S. history in review | Includes glossary, index, and bibliographic information
Identifiers: ISBN 9781978536081 (pbk) | ISBN 9781978536098 (library bound) | ISBN 9781978536104 (ebook)
Subjects: LCSH: Civil rights–Juvenile literature | Constitutional amendments–Juvenile literature | Constitutional history–Juvenile literature | United States– Constitution–1st-10th Amendments–Juvenile literature
Classification: LCC JK40 W35 2024 | DDC 342.73–dc24

Published in 2024 by
Enslow Publishing
2544 Clinton Street
Buffalo, NY 14224

Portions of this work were originally authored by Seth Lynch and published as *The Bill of Rights*. All new material this edition authored by Kathryn Walton.

Designer: Leslie Taylor
Editor: Natalie Humphrey

Photo credits: Cover ungvar/Shutterstock.com; series art (grunge flag) Andrey Kuzmin/Shutterstock.com; series art (stamp icon) Stocker_team/Shutterstock.com; series art (font) santstock/Shutterstock.com; p. 5 Everett Collection/Shutterstock.com; p. 6 Bruce Stanfield/Shutterstock.com; p. 7 Cheryl Casey/Shutterstock.com; p. 8 US Mint; https://commons.wikimedia.org/wiki/File:1993_Bill_of_Rights-Proof_Half_Dollar.jpg; p. 9 Everett Collection/Shutterstock.com; p. 11 Jack R Perry Photography/Shutterstock.com; p. 13 Christopher Penler/Shutterstock.com; p. 14 Bureau of Engraving and Printing/https://commons.wikimedia.org/wiki/File:Religious_Freedom_3c_1957_issue.JPG; p. 15 Richard Thornton/Shutterstock.com; p. 17 Ted Pendergast/Shutterstock.com; p. 19 Alex Photo Stock/Shutterstock.com; p. 21 Maxx-Studio/Shutterstock.com; p. 23 RN Photo Midwest/Shutterstock.com; p. 25 Rawpixel.com/Shutterstock.com; p. 27 Orhan Cam/Shutterstock.com; p. 29 (women suffrage) Suffrage envoys from San Francisco greeted in New Jersey on their way to Washington to present a petition to Congress Suffrage envoys from San Francisco greeted containing more than 500,000 signatures. [Nov.-Dec] Photograph. Retrieved from the Library of Congress, <www.loc.gov/item/mnwp000422/>, (stamp) Solodov Aleksei/Shutterstock.com, (teenager) fitzcrittle/Shutterstock.

Printed in the United States of America

CPSIA compliance information: Batch #CSENS24: For further information, contact Enslow Publishing at 1-800-398-2504.

Contents

A New Beginning 4
Madison Steps In 8
Making the Bill of Rights 10
The First 10 Amendments 12
The Right to Bear Arms 16
The Fourth and Fifth Amendments 18
Due Process 20
The Seventh Amendment 22
Additional Protections 24
The Tenth Amendment 26
The Bill of Rights Today 28
Timeline 30
Glossary 31
For More Information 32
Index 32

*Words in the glossary appear in **bold** the first time they are used in the text.*

A New Beginning

In May 1787, **representatives** from 12 U.S. states met to try and fix the **Articles of Confederation**. They decided that instead of fixing the Articles, they needed a new **constitution**. But some representatives wouldn't agree to the new U.S. Constitution without a promised list of rights.

Learn More

People in favor of ratifying, or agreeing to, the Constitution were called Federalists. People who didn't support the Constitution as it was written were called Anti-Federalists.

George Washington at the Constitutional Convention of 1787

Anti-Federalists worried the new Constitution gave the federal, or national, government too much power. They wanted to add a list of rights to keep the rights of states and **citizens** safe. Many Anti-Federalist leaders would only ratify the **document** with the promise that this list of rights would be added.

Learn More

The promise of a bill of rights stopped Anti-Federalists from further trying to amend, or change, the constitution before it was ratified. After the Federalists made this promise, the Constitution was ratified.

Madison Steps In

James Madison began working on the list of rights to be added. Even though Madison was a Federalist, he was in favor of adding this list to the Constitution. Madison shared his ideas with Congress. Congress decided the Bill of Rights would be its own document.

Learn More

In 1776, George Mason wrote the Virginia Declaration of Rights. James Madison looked at this document for **inspiration** while he wrote the Bill of Rights.

James Madison

Making the Bill of Rights

Madison wrote many **amendments**. The U.S. House of Representatives approved 17 of these amendments. The Senate approved 12 of those amendments in September 1789. Congress sent these to the states. Each amendment needed three-fourths of the states to ratify it to become part of the Constitution.

Learn More

Another way to amend the Constitution is for two-thirds of the states to call for a Constitutional Convention. Any amendments presented would still need to be ratified by three-fourths of the states.

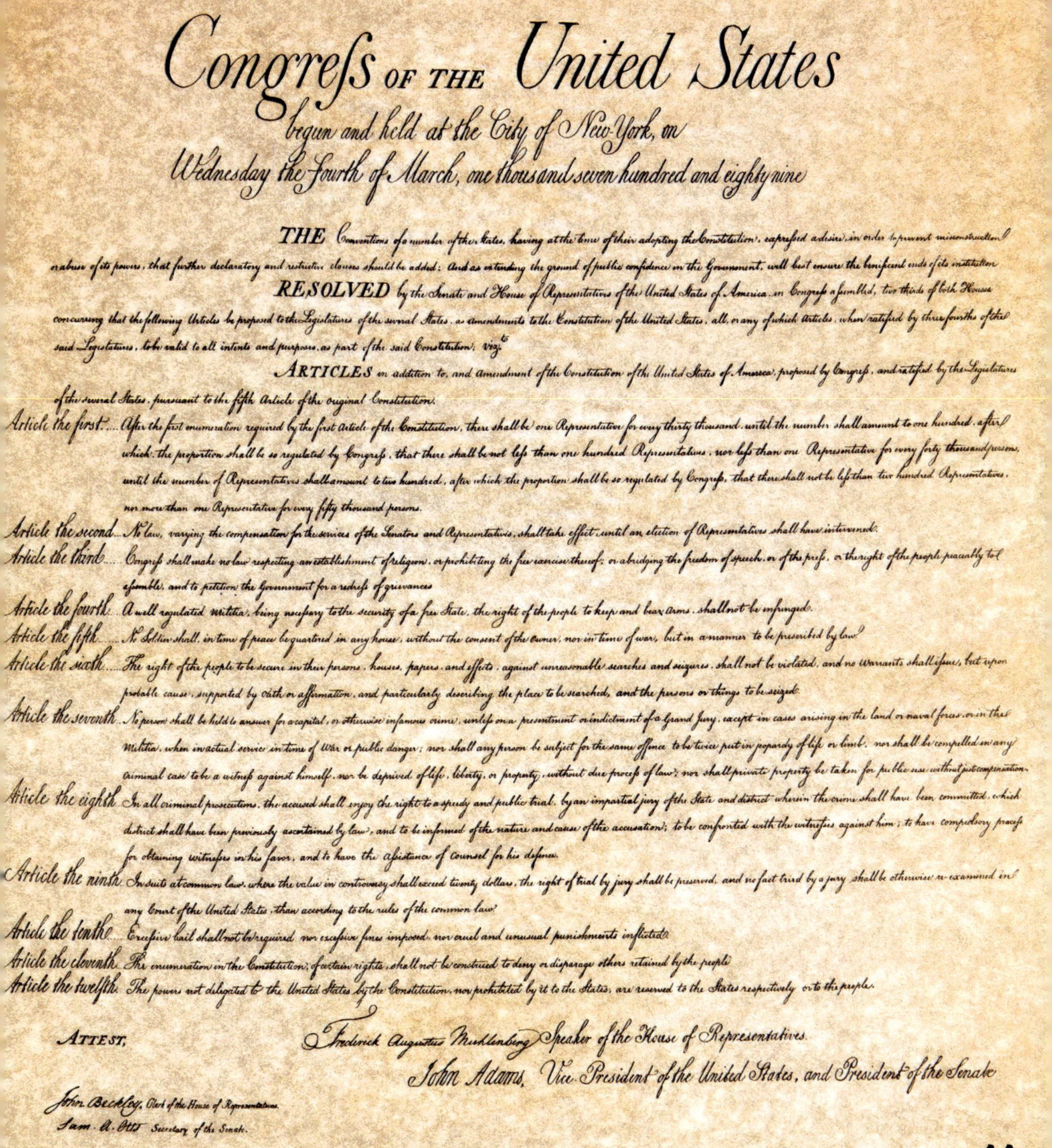

Congrefs of the United States
begun and held at the City of New-York, on
Wednesday the Fourth of March, one thousand seven hundred and eighty nine

THE Conventions of a number of the States, having at the time of their adopting the Constitution, expressed a desire, in order to prevent misconstruction or abuse of its powers, that further declaratory and restrictive clauses should be added: And as extending the ground of public confidence in the Government, will best ensure the beneficent ends of its institution

RESOLVED by the Senate and House of Representatives of the United States of America, in Congress assembled, two thirds of both Houses concurring, that the following Articles be proposed to the Legislatures of the several States, as amendments to the Constitution of the United States, all, or any of which Articles, when ratified by three fourths of the said Legislatures, to be valid to all intents and purposes, as part of the said Constitution; viz.

ARTICLES in addition to, and Amendment of the Constitution of the United States of America, proposed by Congress, and ratified by the Legislatures of the several States, pursuant to the fifth Article of the original Constitution.

Article the first.... After the first enumeration required by the first article of the Constitution, there shall be one Representative for every thirty thousand, until the number shall amount to one hundred, after which the proportion shall be so regulated by Congress, that there shall be not less than one hundred Representatives, nor less than one Representative for every forty thousand persons, until the number of Representatives shall amount to two hundred; after which the proportion shall be so regulated by Congress, that there shall not be less than two hundred Representatives, nor more than one Representative for every fifty thousand persons.

Article the second.... No law, varying the compensation for the services of the Senators and Representatives, shall take effect, until an election of Representatives shall have intervened.

Article the third.... Congress shall make no law respecting an establishment of religion, or prohibiting the free exercise thereof; or abridging the freedom of speech, or of the press; or the right of the people peaceably to assemble, and to petition the Government for a redress of grievances.

Article the fourth.... A well regulated militia, being necessary to the security of a free State, the right of the people to keep and bear arms, shall not be infringed.

Article the fifth.... No Soldier shall, in time of peace be quartered in any house, without the consent of the owner, nor in time of war, but in a manner to be prescribed by law.

Article the sixth.... The right of the people to be secure in their persons, houses, papers, and effects, against unreasonable searches and seizures, shall not be violated, and no warrants shall issue, but upon probable cause, supported by oath or affirmation, and particularly describing the place to be searched, and the persons or things to be seized.

Article the seventh.... No person shall be held to answer for a capital, or otherwise infamous crime, unless on a presentment or indictment of a Grand Jury, except in cases arising in the land or naval forces, or in the militia, when in actual service in time of War or public danger; nor shall any person be subject for the same offence to be twice put in jeopardy of life or limb; nor shall be compelled in any criminal case, to be a witness against himself, nor be deprived of life, liberty, or property, without due process of law; nor shall private property be taken for public use without just compensation.

Article the eighth.... In all criminal prosecutions, the accused shall enjoy the right to a speedy and public trial, by an impartial jury of the State and district wherein the crime shall have been committed, which district shall have been previously ascertained by law, and to be informed of the nature and cause of the accusation; to be confronted with the witnesses against him; to have compulsory process for obtaining witnesses in his favor, and to have the assistance of counsel for his defence.

Article the ninth.... In suits at common law, where the value in controversy shall exceed twenty dollars, the right of trial by jury shall be preserved, and no fact tried by a jury shall be otherwise re-examined in any Court of the United States, than according to the rules of the common law.

Article the tenth.... Excessive bail shall not be required, nor excessive fines imposed, nor cruel and unusual punishments inflicted.

Article the eleventh.... The enumeration in the Constitution, of certain rights, shall not be construed to deny or disparage others retained by the people.

Article the twelfth.... The powers not delegated to the United States by the Constitution, nor prohibited by it to the States, are reserved to the States respectively, or to the people.

ATTEST,

Frederick Augustus Muhlenberg Speaker of the House of Representatives.

John Adams, Vice-President of the United States, and President of the Senate.

John Beckley, Clerk of the House of Representatives.

Sam. A. Otis Secretary of the Senate.

The First 10 Amendments

While 12 amendments went to the states, only 10 were approved. These amendments make up the Bill of Rights. The First Amendment is one of the most important today. It states that citizens have **freedom** of speech and freedom of the press.

Learn More

The First Amendment also protects the right of citizens to gather, or assemble, peacefully. This means people can protest, or strongly disagree with, the government without getting in trouble!

Freedom of belief is also protected, or kept safe, by the First Amendment. This means citizens can believe and practice any religion, or faith, they choose. This was an important right as many people had left Europe looking for religious freedom in America.

Learn More

Under the First Amendment, citizens also have the right to petition, or ask, the government to fix things it may have done wrong.

The Right to Bear Arms

The Second Amendment protects a state's right to a strong **militia**. This amendment states that citizens have a right to "keep and bear arms." Today, this usually means guns, but back then it may have meant swords too!

Learn More

The Third Amendment states that citizens can't be forced to quarter, or keep, soldiers in their homes.

The Fourth and Fifth Amendments

The Fourth Amendment says the government can't take or look through a person's belongings without a **warrant**. The Fifth Amendment protects many different rights. One is that if the government takes a person's **property**, the person must be paid for it.

Learn More

When a person is accused of, or blamed for, breaking the law, the Fourth and Fifth Amendments protect them.

Due Process

The Fifth Amendment also protects a citizen's right to "due process of law." This means that a set of laws must be followed when someone is accused of a crime. The laws are supposed to make sure the person is treated fairly.

Learn More

The Sixth Amendment protects the right to a "speedy and public" trial. A trial is a meeting in court where a judge and **jury** learn about a case and make decisions based on the law.

The Seventh Amendment

The Seventh Amendment talks about civil cases, or cases that are just between people. Civil cases are tried by a jury if the property in question is worth more than $20. In the Eighth Amendment, citizens are also protected from "cruel and unusual punishment."

Learn More

The Eighth Amendment also talks about bail, or the money that people can pay to be freed from jail before their trial. It states citizens shouldn't have to pay large fines or bail.

Additional Protections

The Ninth Amendment isn't as clear as the other amendments. It states that citizens have rights not included in the Bill of Rights. It's meant to stop the federal government from increasing its power and to protect other citizens' rights.

A crowd of protesters gathers to protect their rights.

Learn More

James Madison wrote other amendments that didn't make it into the Bill of Rights, but it's not clear what other rights he might have wanted to protect.

The Tenth Amendment

The Tenth Amendment is also more general than the other amendments. It says that any power that isn't given to the federal government by the Constitution is given to the states or to the citizens of the United States.

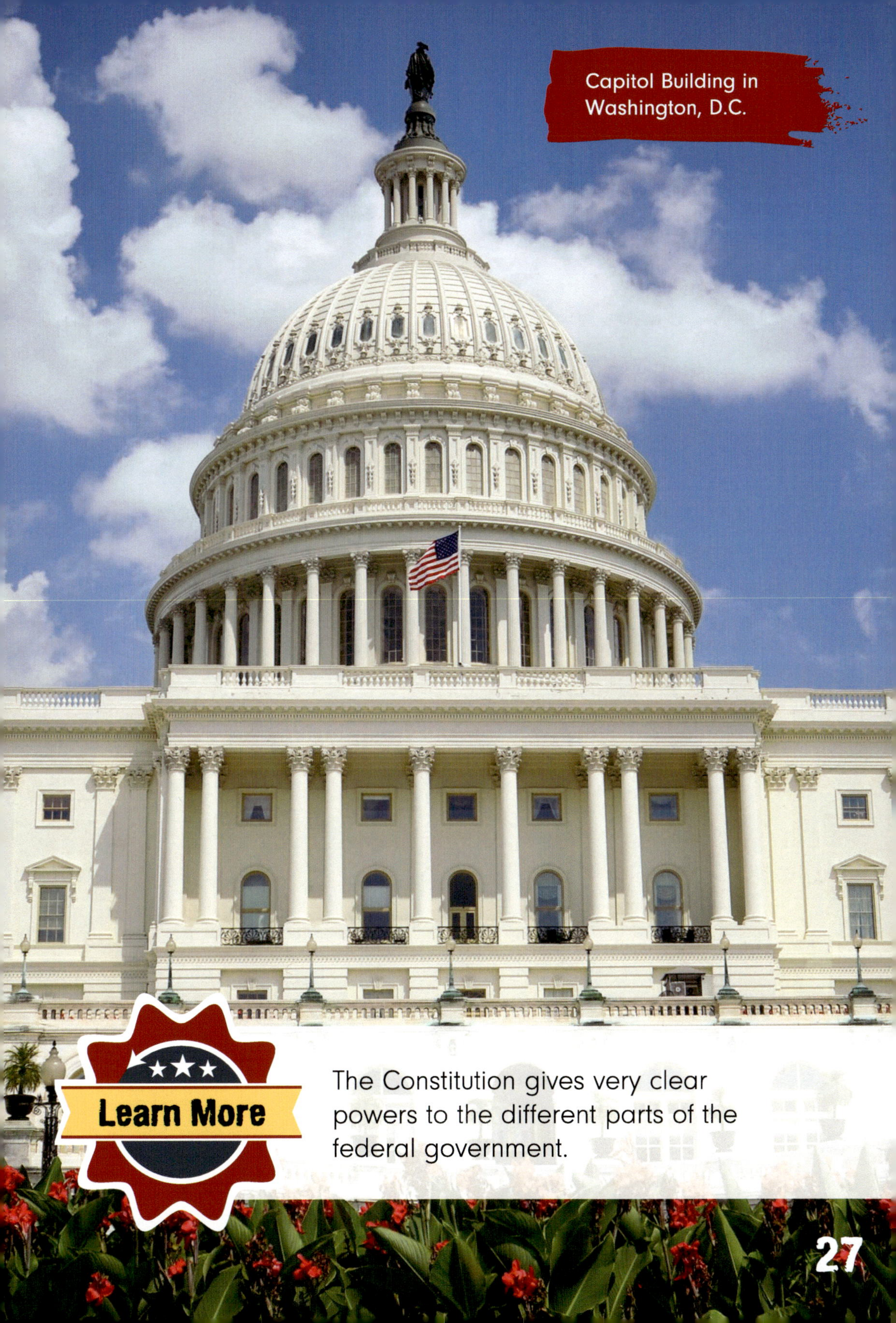

Capitol Building in Washington, D.C.

Learn More

The Constitution gives very clear powers to the different parts of the federal government.

The Bill of Rights Today

Since the Bill of Rights was ratified, many more amendments have been added to the Constitution. While these new amendments aren't part of the Bill of Rights, they're still important! These new amendments help make the government run smoother and protect more rights of citizens.

Learn More

The 13th Amendment guaranteed freedom for enslaved people across the United States. The 19th Amendment gave women the right to vote. The 26th Amendment states anyone 18 or older can vote!

Timeline

March 1, 1781
The Articles of Confederation, the first constitution of the United States, is ratified by the states.

September 3, 1783
The signing of the Treaty of Paris ends the American Revolution.

May 25, 1787
The Constitutional Convention, at which a new U.S. Constitution is written, begins.

June 1788
Enough states ratify the Constitution, making it the highest law in the land.

June 8, 1789
James Madison presents changes to the Constitution to Congress.

September 25, 1789
A set of 12 amendments protecting states' and citizens' rights are presented to the states.

December 15, 1791
The Bill of Rights is ratified as 10 amendments.

Glossary

amendment: A change or addition to a constitution.

Articles of Confederation: The document that created the first central government of the United States in 1777.

citizen: Someone who lives in a country legally and has certain rights.

constitution: The basic laws by which a country or state is governed.

document: A formal piece of writing.

freedom: The power to do what you want to do.

inspiration: Something that inspires, or gives someone an idea of what to do, make, or think.

jury: A group of people that comes together to judge a trial.

militia: A group of citizens who organize like soldiers in order to protect themselves or an area.

property: All the things a person owns including belongings and land.

representative: A member of a lawmaking body who acts for voters.

warrant: A document signed by a judge and given to a police officer that gives the officer the right to do something.

For More Information

Books

Levy, Janey. *The Bill of Rights: Guaranteeing Liberty.* Buffalo, NY: Gareth Stevens Publishing, 2021.

Schaefer, Benjamin Mark. *What Are States' Rights?* Buffalo, NY: Gareth Stevens Publishing, 2022.

Website

America's Story from America's Library
www.americaslibrary.gov/jb/nation/jb_nation_bofright_1.html
Discover more about the history of the Bill of Rights.

Publisher's note to educators and parents: *Our editors have carefully reviewed this website to ensure that it is suitable for students. Many websites change frequently, however, and we cannot guarantee that a site's future contents will continue to meet our high standards of quality and educational value. Be advised that students should be closely supervised whenever they access the internet.*

Index

amendments, 12, 13, 14, 15, 16, 17, 18, 19, 20, 21, 22, 23, 24, 25, 26, 28, 29
American Revolution, 30
Anti-Federalists, 5, 6, 7
Articles of Confederation, 4, 30
Congress, 8, 10, 30
Constitutional Convention, 5, 11, 30
due process, 20
Federalists, 5, 7, 8
Madison, James, 8, 9, 25, 30
ratify, 5, 6, 10, 11, 28, 30
Washington, George, 5